These Are the Things We Found by the Sea

My Mommy, My Mama, My Brother, and Me

Words by **Natalie Meisner**
Art by **Mathilde Cinq-Mars**

NIMBUS
PUBLISHING LTD.
— NIMBUS.CA —

Nimbus Publishing Limited
3660 Strawberry Hill Street, Halifax, NS, B3K 5A9
(902) 455-4286 nimbus.ca

Printed and bound in Canada

NB1357

Editor: Whitney Moran
Proofreader: Penelope Jackson
Design: Heather Bryan

Library and Archives Canada Cataloguing in Publication

Title: These are the things we found by the sea : my mommy, my mama,
my brother, & me / words by Natalie Meisner ; art by Mathilde Cinq-Mars
Other titles: My mommy, my mama, my brother, and me
Names: Meisner, Natalie D., 1972- author. | Cinq-Mars, Mathilde, 1988- illustrator.
Identifiers: Canadiana (print) 20189068159 |
Canadiana (ebook) 20189068167 | ISBN 9781771087414
(hardcover) | ISBN 9781771087421 (HTML)
Classification: LCC PS8576.E433 T54 2019 | DDC jC813/.54—dc23

Nimbus Publishing acknowledges the financial support for its publishing activities from the
Government of Canada, the Canada Council for the Arts, and from the Province of Nova
Scotia. We are pleased to work in partnership with the Province of Nova Scotia to develop and
promote our creative industries for the benefit of all Nova Scotians.

My home is a town surrounded by sea

The bank, school, post office,
My family, and me

That house is ours
Last one by the dock
Come in for a visit
Don't bother to knock

We're used to the fog
Here, it's thick like pea soup
If you like, you can taste it
Come have a scoop!

Then, all of a sudden
The sun reappears
Soon we'll have sand
From our toes to our ears!

Our town has a beach
Just up over the hill
And whenever we go
We bring buckets to fill

The beach waits for us
With waves like green glass
We run on the sand
We hide in long grass

And these are the things we find by the sea
My mommy, my mama, my brother, and me.

lobster claw

plover nest

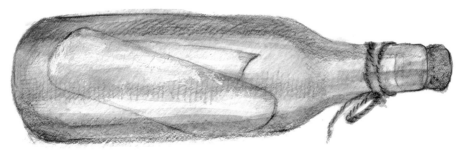

note in a bottle

we can't keep them all
So each day we choose
One thing to cherish
The rest, we let loose

See the fisherfolk, there
Hauling their nets?
They've caught something
Tasty for dinner, I bet

Out on the water are colourful floats
Stripes, dots, and patterns for every boat
They each have their own so they don't get confused
About which one is what one and whose trap is whose

And these are the things we find by the sea
My mommy, my mama, my brother, and me.

Come over here, quick
And see what I've found:
Hard, black, and shiny—
On top, smooth and round

The tip's sharp and pointy
It feels just like leather
Yet dry to the touch
And light as a feather

Is this a plant?
A seaweed of some kind?
It doesn't feel hollow—
Is something inside?

Here comes our neighbour
Captain Enslow
Let's show it to him
And see if he knows.

This here's what they call a mermaid's purse
Inside's an egg of a shark, like a nurse
a sharpnose, a dusky, a tiger-or maybe,
perhaps it's a sting ray-if you look inside 'er.

Take it on home
Give it a salt bath
If a baby's in there
You might see him hatch.

So I wade in the ocean and fill up my pail.
Mind you, change the water
So it doesn't go stale

Let me know what comes out,
Could be something quite rare.
And he waves to my moms
As he tousles my hair.

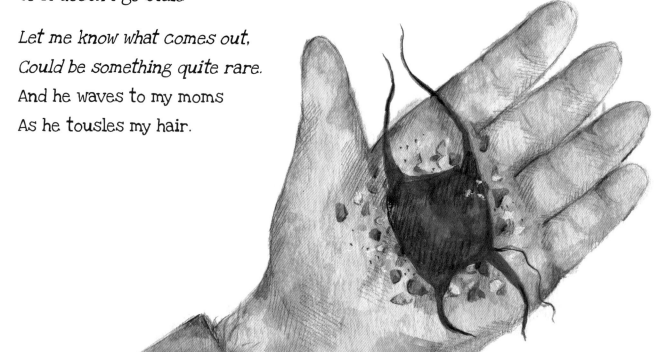

And these are the things we find by the sea
My mommy, my mama, my brother, and me.

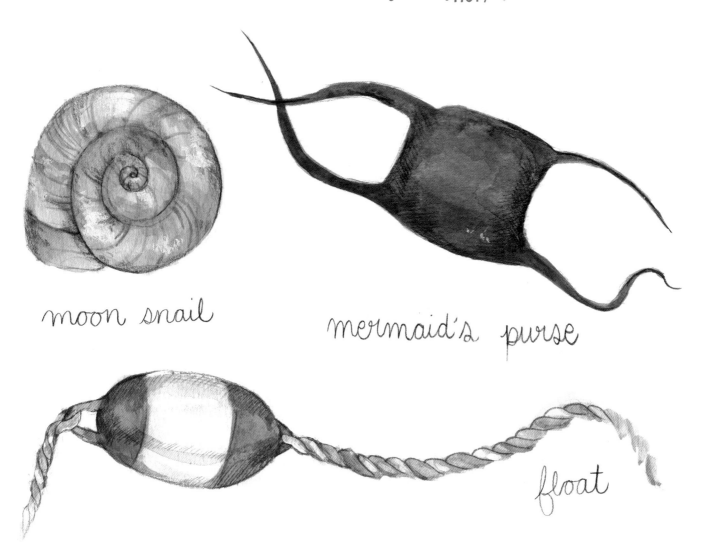

moon snail

mermaid's purse

float

Miss Poole paints a picture each and every day
Of the beach and the sea
Yet they're never the same

She walks the whole shoreline
No matter the weather
With her little dog, Boots
They're always together

Today she arrives with a gift in her hand
It glows like a fire as she brushes off sand.

I've found something special, says Miss Poole
Something you don't often find, as a rule
Think of the bonfire this glass melted in
How it hardened from heat and was sanded again
To a smooth misty finish by each grain of sand
As it rolled in the waves when the tides came in.

We ask if she wants it
She smiles and says, *No*
You keep it; I'll paint it
Come on, Boots, let's go

And these are the things we find by the sea
My mommy, my mama, my brother, and me.

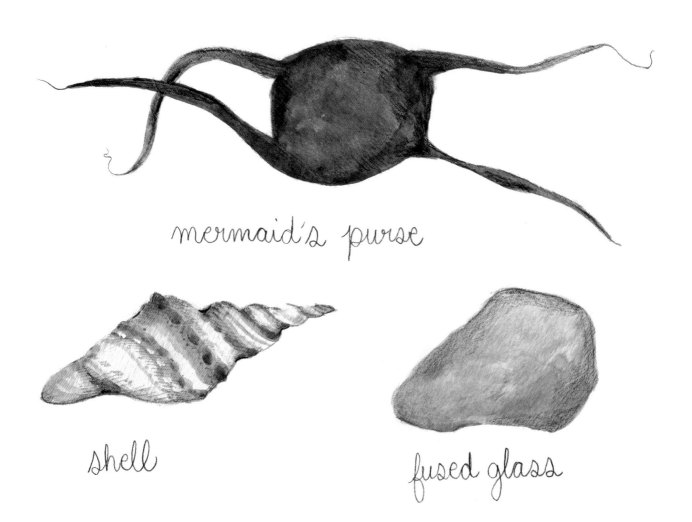

mermaid's purse

shell

fused glass

My brother finds something that looks like a pickle
It's green with white speckles
And covered with prickles

We're not sure what it is
But hey, we're in luck
Along comes the man everybody calls Buck

He knows all the creatures
That live under the sea
He has walls of books about biology

He says, *Good day! What you've got there's an urchin*
Used to be common—
We'd find 'em without searchin'!

Folks here don't eat them
But they're tasty, you see
And in faraway lands they're a delicacy!

Inside the shell it's orangey-yellow.
This part is called uni, my curious fellow
He says, *You can eat it if you're feeling spry.*
And Mama says, *You never know till you try.*

So I do and the taste is hard to describe
It's sweet and it's salty all at the same time
But I like it, I think
And I'm glad that I tried

And these are the things we find by the sea
My mommy, my mama, my brother, and me.

fused glass

starfish

urchin

When we get to the end of the beach, we stop
For a picnic lunch by our favourite flat rock

Mama points out to sea
As the boats come in
See *how they're followed by "the fisherman's friend"?*
The parts of a fish we can't eat go to them

The gulls make it their job to clean up the sea
This keeps the beach fine for you and for me

Something else about seagulls
That's really unique
They're the only creatures
Who can drink the sea!
The salt doesn't hurt them
It comes out through their beak!

And these are the things we find by the sea
My mommy, my mama, my brother, and me.

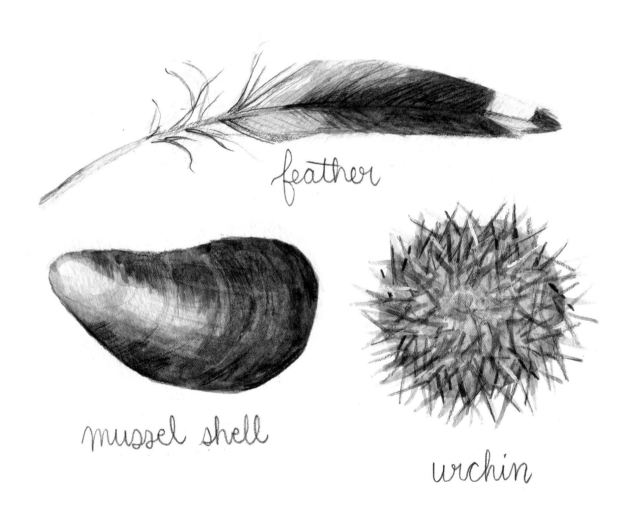

feather

mussel shell

urchin

Now comes the hard part of a day by the sea
Mama hugs us and asks my brother and me

Of all of our treasures
And all of our bounty
What is the thing
That we most want to keep?

A long white feather
A shell from the deep?
Rare beach glass
Or uni, fresh from the sea?

My brother and I sit down in the sun
When thinking, two heads are better than one

This day's been astounding, amazing, first-rate
Just top-notch and wonderful...
So, what made it that way?

It wasn't the things that we found on the ground
It was the people we talked to, the new friends we found

And we run to our moms and we say, *Now we know!*
Just what it is we most want to take home...

Not the beach glass
   or shells
      or the salty seafoam
         It's the neighbours we spoke with
           who shared what *they* know.

And these are the **friends**
we found by the sea...

My mommy, my mama,
my brother, and me.

A Note from the Author

Ihad the great good fortune to grow up in a Nova Scotia fishing community with the beach, tide pools, and shoreline as my playground. The beach was where you learned about the dangers of water, practiced balance by leaping boulders, and met your neighbours. You learned about life, death, and mystery as you found creatures or mysterious objects washed up on the tideline. We also had something else: community. A network of individuals who taught us things and cared about us as we grew up.

The beauty of rural places is that we really do have an entire village cheering for us from the sidelines, offering encouragement, a sandwich, or a good piece of advice. One of the downsides of these places, however, is that they can sometimes be less accepting of family structures or individuals who fall outside the traditional. One of the reasons I felt I had to leave the small village where I grew up is that I thought I would never be accepted as an artist, a lesbian, a gender-fluid person... but I have discovered this is far from the case.

My wife and I lived in Lockeport, Nova Scotia, where I grew up, when our babies were born. Our two boys took their first steps on Crescent Beach. Our family model (we are a biracial, two-mom family) was likely unfamiliar to most and yet the arms of the town opened to us and have remained open as our sons grow up. If they had never encountered a family like ours before, they did not let that stop them. I hope this book will help with community building and spreading the word about diverse families, all while being gentle and fun, and taking inspiration from the mysterious offerings of the seashore.

Acknowledgements

To my wife, Viviën, and sons, Jasper and Ruben, for lighting up every day with wonder. To my mom, Yolanda, Opa and Oma, aunties, uncles, cousins, friends, and neighbours for loving us in all our difference. To Bev Rach and Dr. Sharon Smulders for early creative suggestions and inspiration. To Whitney Moran, Mathilde Cinq-Mars, and everyone at Nimbus for bringing the book to life in an even more beautiful way than I saw in my mind's eye.

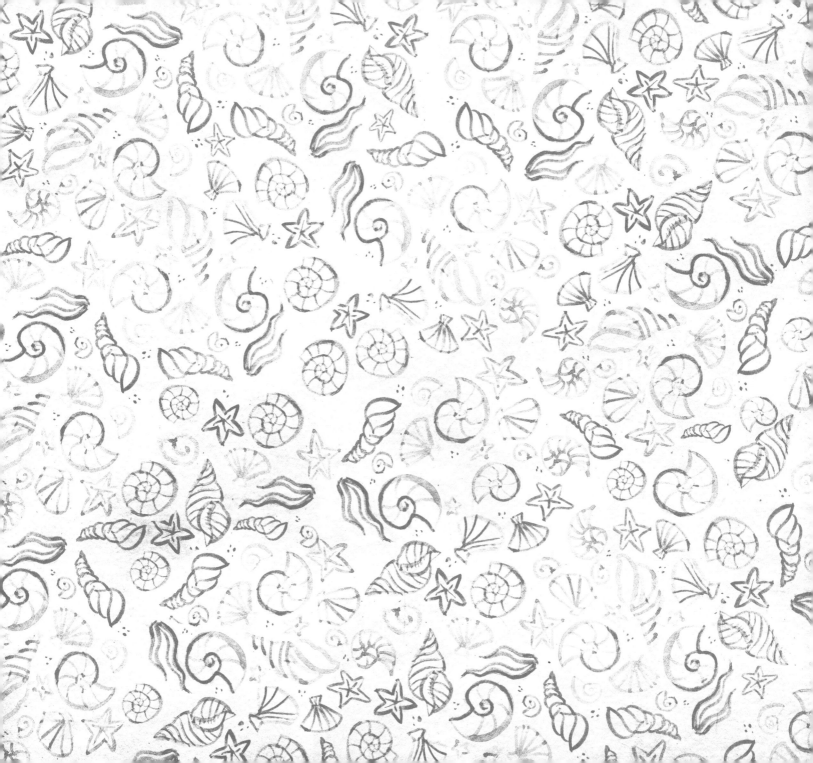